For my two bo
Adam & Killian

Written By - Gary O'B rien
Illustrated By: Caitriona Dalton

"Are you ready for today, my dear?" Dana's father asked as they sat down to breakfast.

"I'm so ready Dad," she said.

Today was Dana's 250th Bloomday. That's like being twelve in our world. Now she was old enough to take a seat on the elven council, just like her dad.

Today was special for another reason. It was the day a magical gem, called the Coridwen Ruby would appear in the land of Allaria. This magical gem appeared only once a year, and if captured would supply power and protection to the elven village for the year ahead.

The task of capturing the Ruby fell to one lucky elf, this year that elf was Dana.

"I'm sure you will do great," said her father. "But remember my advice!"

"I will, Dad. I promise." She said.

"Happy Bloomday my dear," said her mother, kissing her on the cheek. "Your father and I got you a small gift." She took a small box wrapped in bright paper from beneath her apron.

Dana's eyes lit up.

"Oh, thank you so much," she gushed as she tore it open.

Inside the box sat a shiny gold disc. Dana's hands shook with excitement as she flipped open the lid.

"We thought this would come in useful today," said her father.

Inside the disc was a beautiful gold compass.

"Look there is an inscription inside," said her mother.

Dana read it aloud. *"Find Your Own Direction." It read.*

It's wonderful she said giving them both the biggest hug.

Just then there was a rap on the door. Dana rushed to see if it was her friends, Bran and Aoife.

They had been her closest friends since they were all in kindergarten. They had been on many adventures together and never missed each others bloomday.

But, it was only the post.

Dana was disappointed, as she shuffled through the post, hoping for a card.

"Nope," she said as she lay the post on the table.

"It's all for you guys," she muttered to her parents feeling disappointed.

Had her friends forgotten? She thought.

"You'd better go get ready," said her Father as he rose to leave.

Dana packed her bag and compass and said goodbye to her Mum.

"Stay safe my love", said her mother. "And good Luck."

Dana flew down to the village below, on her way she passed Aoife's house.

"I wonder if she is home," she thought.

"Maybe I should call in and say hi."

The door was open, and Dana poked her head in.

"Hello, Aoife!" She called out.

Aoife's mother heard the call and came out.

"Hello, Dana, I'm sorry but Aoife is not here now. She left early this morning and I've no idea where she 's got to."

Dana gave a weak smile and sighed.

"Ok, thanks Mrs. Alerion. I'm sure I will see her later." She said turning to leave.

As she neared the Town-hall, Dana felt very glum, until she saw Bran waiting on the steps outside.

"Hey there Dana," he said loudly, clapping her on the shoulder.

"Are you ready for today, have you studied the texts?"

"Yes!" Sighed Dana, "I've read the text's and I've spoken to the other elves who've hunted the Ruby in the past.

I'm ready."

She looked at him with confusion on her face. Had he also forgotten her bloomday?

He didn't seem to notice and said, "I'll walk in with you, the council members are all assembled.

Bran followed Dana though the Town-hall, towards the council chamber. As they walked Dana's mind was full of questions like...

Why was Bran here?

Why had all her friends forgotten her bloomday?

Her mind was definitely not on the task ahead.

"Last year on his bloomday I made him that new knife," thought Dana.

"And he has carried it with him everyday since. And I made that beautiful glass owl for Aoife of her bloomday too. How could they forget me like this"?

A very distracted and unhappy Dana stepped into the council chamber, the Coridwen Ruby far from her mind.

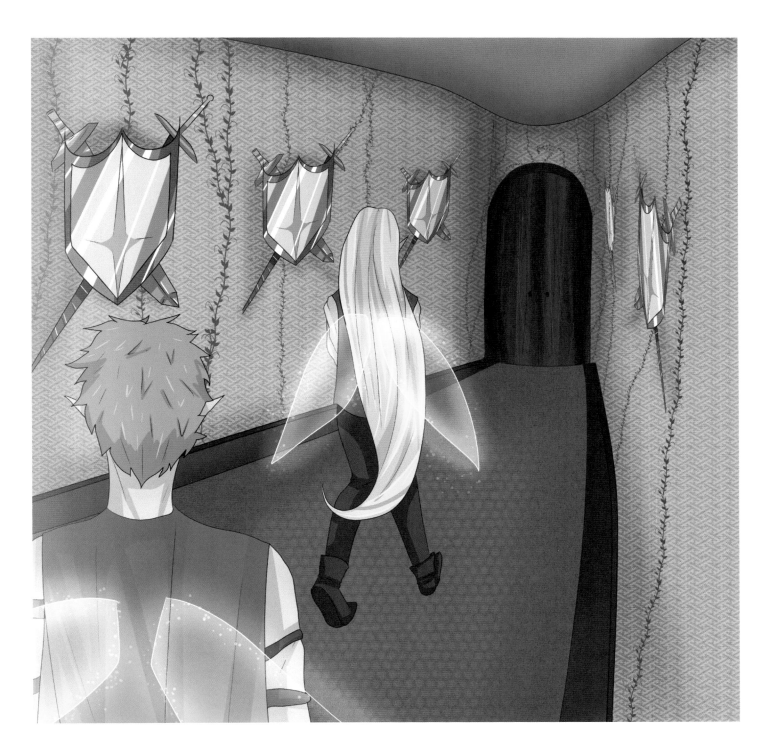

At the top of the room on a dais stood three wooden thrones. Above the center throne hung a replica of the Coridwen Ruby.

A door opened to the right and in walked three of the council Elders.

First came Elder zPret Alerion. He was Aoife's grandfather and the oldest of the elves, at eight hundred and seventy-six years old. Making him about seventy three years old in our years.

He took up his position on the center throne.

Elder Indani Cerbaun was next. She was Bran's mother. And she sat on the throne to the left of center. Finally, out walked Elder Larpraz Idesan, Dana's father, who took his place in the last seat.

Each of the Elders nodded toward Dana.

Dana and Bran bowed in return.

Elder zPret was the first to speak.

"Welcome young elf Dana Idesan, on this very special day. Today, on your 250th Bloomday, you must fulfill the task of Dúshlán.

Many centuries ago, the Great Warrior elf Dús first discovered the Coridwen Ruby's power. And every year since one elf on their bloomday, must repeat his success.

They must prove themselves worthy of a place on this council."

Dana stood expressionless as Elder zPret spoke.

She was only partial listening to him.

"Why are you here?" Dana whispered to Bran.

"I don't know, I was just asked to attend this morning." He replied.

A sharp cough from Elder Indani caught their attention.

Elder zPret was sitting, staring at them, frowning.

"There are three possible locations the Ruby will appear." He continued.

The first, is the great cave of Cadair Fomor.

Not only is the cave dark and full of deep caverns and pits, were a distracted young elf could easily get lost." He said raising an eyebrow in Dana's direction.

"But here also lurks the Giant Idris Fomor.
He is a ruthless tyrant, who will defend the ruby to the last.
Many a young elf has gone in there never to return.

Bran swallowed loudly at this.

"Shh… Muttered Dana, throwing him her best 'Not Impressed Look.'

She glanced next to her father. He just looked blankly ahead and did not even acknowledge her. So, she reset her attention on Elder zPret.

"The next location you may find the Ruby", he continued. "Is at the center of the Craven Marsh. It is said that it is easy to enter, but much harder to leave.

A place of confusion and mystery.

Some of our brothers and sisters have returned from there frightened out of their minds.

Some have not spoken since.

Others say the Marsh is haunted by foul beasts, and winged dragons.

You must keep your wits about you at all times, young elf.

Finally, the last possible place you may find the Coridwen Ruby is on the Emerald Lake.

It is to the south of the Wasted Lands.

There are over twenty islands on the lake, and you may have to search all of them. It will pay to be mindful of the time.

Also they are protected by wicked wind and water sprites only the smartest elf can possibly outwit them.

Are you a smart elf, young Dana Idesan?" He asked.

"Yes, I think so your grace," she replied.

"I will not let you down, good council," Dana said with such conviction that no-one could have doubted her.

"I will return by sunrise with the gem."

"Your courage is to be admired; may the graces of Dús go with you." declared Indani.

"Make your way to the supply store my child," spoke Dana's father.

"Take what you feel you will need for your journey but remember pick wisely, as useless items will only slow you down."

He gestured to a door on his left as the other Elders left the chamber.

As Dana left the room, she turned back to see Bran and her father huddled together talking.

"What could they possibly be scheming?" She thought

"Hey hold up!" shouted Bran as he trotted over to catch up.

"What was that about?" She asked him as he joined her in the storeroom.

"Oh nothing, just village security matters," he replied absently.

The room was full of all sorts of items. Weapons, armour, food, fabric and even some magic potions, all laid out on rows of tables.

Dana grabbed a small shard of Cactus, a small cotton vest, a ball of twine, a waterproof sheet made from the leaves of a rubber tree, and a small square mirror.

"Aren't you going to take a weapon?" asked Bran. "From what Elder zPret described you might need one."

"I'm happy with my slingshot, and my wits," she replied.

"Now where to first?" she asked herself aloud as she stood looking up at a map of Allaria.

"It looks like the Craven Marsh is closest to Ninor," said Bran. "And I've heard it's not a great place to be after sunset either. Perhaps it would be best to start there. Plus, that's where the Ruby's been found the last two years."

"I agree," said Dana.

"Your pony, Ramira is ready for you, down at the stable." Said Bran as he held the door open.

"Wish me luck." said Dana as she left.

"Good Luck!" He shouted after her.

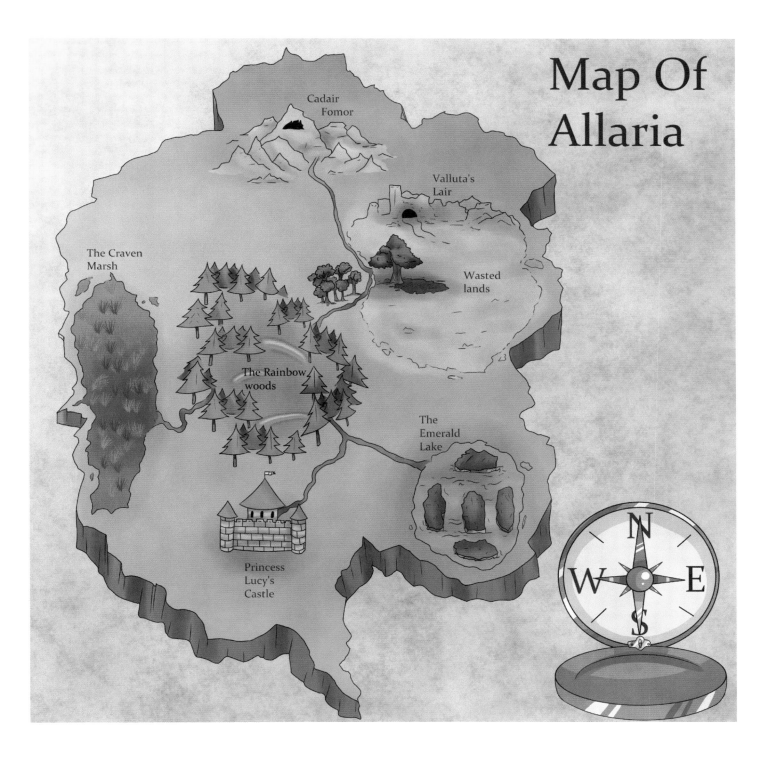

Dana and Ramira set off through the rainbow woods. Many of the villagers waved her off, as she passed by.

"Good luck." some shouted.

"Bring back the Ruby," shouted others.

Shortly she came to a junction in the road. The signpost read, south towards the castle and west to the Craven Marsh.

Dana clicked her heels and said, "Come on Ramira, we'll show those so called friends we don't need them." and they trotted out the western road.

As she neared the Craven Marsh, the first thing she noticed was the fog that hung love over the islands of grass.

It was so thick it blocked out most of the sun. But off in the distance a pulsating red light glowed through the gloom.

"That must be the Ruby," she thought.

"This will be easy!"

Dana pulled the compass from her pack and finding north she could see the glow was off to the north west.

"Keep an eye out for the deep bog holes. Stick to the grass islands." came the voice of her father inside her head.

"The Craven Marsh is dark and full of deep watery holes where an unsuspecting elf could get lost. It's a dangerous place." She had read in one of the Coridwen Ruby textbooks from the Warrior Dús.

As she moved deeper into the marsh, Dana caught a glimpse of a shadow darting across the path ahead of her.

"What was that?" She cried out, startled.

A sense of panic began to rise in her chest.

There it was again, this time it was closer. Whatever it was it appeared to have wings.

A howling screech shattered the silence.

Dana froze on the spot. Everything seems to be moving closer and further away at the same time.

Just as she was about to pass out, she remembered something she had read about the fog, and reached for her bag.

Dana pulled out the shard of Cactus and cotton vest she had taken from the storeroom earlier.

She cracked the shard and crushed it over the vest, until the juice soaked it.

Then with a great effort she tied it around her mouth and nose and took several slow deep breaths.

Slowly the flying shadows lost their menace.

As her mind cleared she saw them for what they actually were.

Just dancing fireflies.

She looked around for the red glow, but unfortunately it had gone too.

"Not so easy after all!" She muttered.

Disappointed she turned back to face south east and headed out of the marsh.

Once back on the road, Dana decided to head for the Emerald Lake. It was much closer than climbing into the mountains of Cadair Fomor.

Before long she could see the castle across the fields. This was where her friend Princess Lucy lived.

"I bet, Lucy hasn't forgotten my bloomday," thought Dana.

"She's a good friend and always happy to see me. Maybe I should call in and say hi! After all there is still plenty of time left in the day."

As she reached the castle entrance, Dana tied Ramira to a post and gave her a handful of oats from her bag.

As she turned to enter the castle a rushing figure knocked her to the ground.

"Watch out!" She said as she stood and dusted herself off.

"Oh! Dana, I'm so sorry, I didn't see you there." Said Princess Lucy blushing.

"Where are you off to in such a hurry?" Dana said frowning.

"Eh-em… I'm off to see Adora the Unicorn, sorry can't stay, got to go, bye!"

Princess Lucy rushed off down the road towards the Rainbow Woods.

"Humph," said Dana.

It seemed like another friend had forgotten her special day.

As she neared the lake the wind was getting stronger. The trees were small and like old men they were bent in the force of it.

Up ahead she saw the first glint of light shining on the water surface.

The Emerald lake was vast, and it was dotted with different sized islands.

"This won't be a problem," said Dana.

"I'll just fly out over the islands and look out for the Ruby's glow. If it's here it will be easy to find."

Dana left Ramira grazing and launched herself into the sky.

A large wind sprite appeared before her and with a sudden gust of wind blew her back onto the shore with a thump.

"Let's try that again!" She said darting out over the water. Here the wind did not seem as strong.

Just then a water sprite popped it's head out of the waves and began spraying water into Dana's face.

"Ugh! Stop it I can't see" she yelled as she flew in circles.

But it was useless, she found herself back at the shore, dripping wet.

"Now that's a problem." She thought.

"How am I to get to the islands if they're so heavily guarded?

Just then she remembered one of the inventions she had been working on. She ran to Ramira and opened her bag.

Dana took out the sheet of woven leaves, the length of twine and the small square mirror, she had taking from the town-hall.

She gathered a bundle of fallen twigs and removed the pane of glass from the mirror and hurriedly assembled all the pieces.

The result looked like a miniature hot air balloon.

"I need something to weigh it down," she muttered looking around her.

"Oh, these will do just fine." She said, as she found some rocks at the base of an overhang.

Tying the rocks around the base of the balloon, she placed it over her head, and walked out into the water hoping it would work.

Once she was beneath the waves, she was able to walk along the lake-bed without issue. Her balloon contraption keeping the air in and the water out.

Off in the distance Dana spotted a faint red glow.

"The Ruby!" she whispered.

But walking through water was slow going and after what felt like a long time to her, it didn't seem to be getting any closer.

Then, like a flash the Ruby was gone.

"Not again! All that effort for nothing. I'm cold, and wet on my bloomday. My friends didn't even remember. What's the point?" She thought.

She cut the rocks away from the diving balloon and slowly rose to the surface, where a particularly grumpy wind sprite blew her right back to shore.

Dana found that a small fire pit had been prepared close to where she had tied Ramira.

"I don't recall that being there before." She thought, and quickly looked to see if anyone else was about.

Something moved in the bushes. Dana pulled out her slingshot and roared. "Come out, no point in hiding. I know you're there."

But no-one came out, and there were no further movements.

She lit the fire and prepared a little food while her clothes dried.

It was getting late in the day, almost mid-afternoon, and her last chance to catch the Coridwen Ruby lay several hours to the north, in the home of Idris Fomor the giant.

"I was hoping to avoid this one," she said to Ramira as they set off again.

As she passed the orchard and came upon the Wasted Lands, she recalled the adventure she'd shared with her friends, Aoife, Bran, and Princess Lucy.

They had taken on the wicked Dark Elf Valutta to rescue Adora the unicorn.

"Those had been happier times," she thought.

Where were her friends now?

Especially on her bloomday!

Feeling very lonely Dana wiped away the tears that trickled down her face and spurred Ramira onward into the mountains.

At last they reached the foot of Mount Cadair Fomor.

The sun was sitting along the ridge, as nighttime was closing in.

Dana pulled on her bag and with a deep inhale of breath she started to climb up the slope.

One of the fading rays of sunlight flashed on something blue ahead.

She caught a glimpse of it as it dashed across the path causing a small cascade of loose rocks to tumble down the hill toward her.

When she finally resumed her climb, whatever or whoever caused it had gone.

Two torches hung either side of the cave entrance, their light shone brightly of the highly polished floor.

Dana grabbed a small branch from a bush and wrapped a scrap of the cotton vest around one end.

Lighting it she slowly made her way into the cave.

All was quiet within, apart from a distant plink, plink of water dripping somewhere in the darkness.

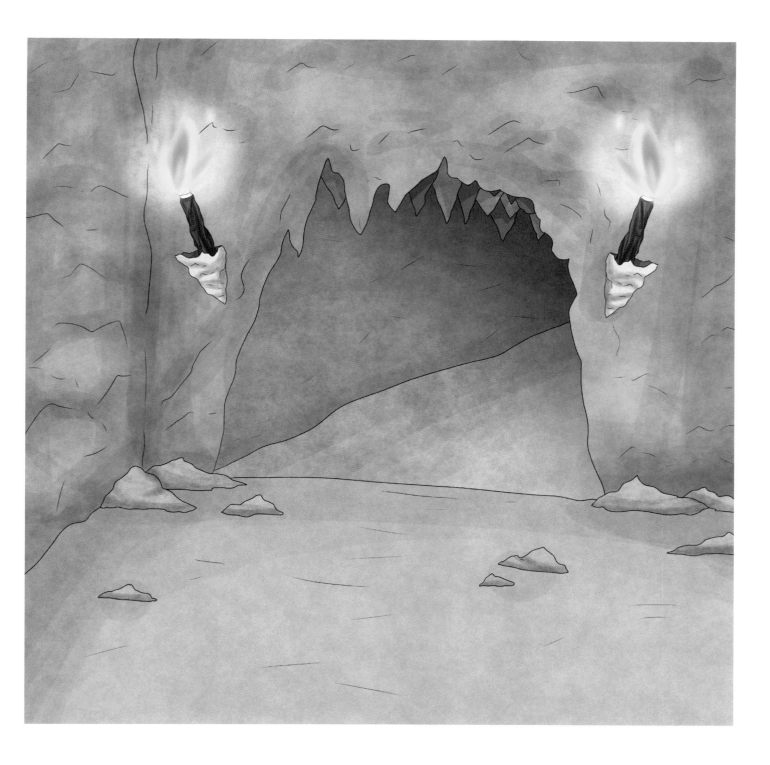

Shortly Dana came across two tunnels. One led down, deep into the earth and the other climbed upward.

"Which way to go?" She wondered.

She began reciting and old poem from school. Something to do with tigers and toes, when a sudden flash of red light filled the doorway of the downward tunnel.

She moved quietly down the steps towards the source of the light.

She could hear a low rumble, coming from deep within.

"Sounds like my Dad snoring," Dana thought with a grin.

Up ahead was a high arched doorway, the glow was much brighter here.

"I won't need this now," she said, placing the torch in an empty brazier on the wall.

Peeking her head slowly around the corner the source of the rumble immediately became clear.

Sitting on the biggest stone chair she'd ever seen; was the biggest person she'd ever seen.

Idris Fomor was sleeping deeply and just to his left sat the radiant Coridwen Ruby. It filled the cavern with its bright red glow.

"It is more beautiful than I ever imagined," Dana sighed.

It sat high above a mound of emeralds, sapphires, and diamonds.

"How can I get up there?" She wondered.

"I will have to climb, it's far to risky to fly up there with all these pointy rocks hanging from the ceiling."

As she crept closer, Dana noticed the enormous club lying across the giant's lap.

His equally enormous hairy hand rested gently across it.

"I wouldn't like to get hit with that," she was thinking when suddenly...

Her foot kicked an emerald the size of a lime across the cave floor.

She looked down at it and then back up at the sleeping Giant.

In a split second the Giant's club came crashing down just where she had been standing.

She had managed to dive behind a row of rocks and hid in the darkness.

"I know you are there, Elf! I smell your sweet sickly floral scent..." Roared Idris Fomor.

"You've come to steal the Ruby, have you? You'll not leave here this night," he bellowed.

Dana slowly crept from behind the row of rocks, staying close to the cave wall in the shadows as she went.

"He has gone very quiet," she thought.

Suddenly the giant's head appeared. He reached a hairy arm out into the darkness grabbing wildly at the air in front of her.

She could feel the hot, foul gusts of his breath in her face.

"How shall I ever get out of here," she thought frantically.

Then, suddenly out of nowhere, there was a crash of rocks somewhere deep in the cave. Idris Fomor twisted his head and roared as he stomped off toward it.

"You'll not escape from me." He howled.

"How lucky…" said Dana.

"Now is my chance."

She ran up the pile of gems and hovered before the blazing Ruby.

"It is beautiful," she whispered awestruck.

Then quick as a flick she grabbed her prize and stowed it safely into her bag and hurried back the way she came.

There had been no other sign of Idris Fomor after that. Just the odd crash of boulders somewhere off deep in the caves, followed by angry roars.

Dana flew down from the cave entrance, landing in Ramira's saddle.

They galloped as fast as the pony's legs could go.

Back past the Wasted Lands. Past the Orchard and into the Rainbow Woods.

And finally to the safety of Ninor.

As she approached the town much of the village was in darkness.

But there, standing outside the doors of the town-hall was her father and Bran.

As she dismounted Bran bowed to Larpraz and ducked inside the hall.

"Welcome back my good daughter," he said smiling, as he stepped forward to embrace her.

"Have you been successful?" he whispered.

"Yes, Father." She said, still out of breath.

"I told you, I would not let you down," she said pulling the Coridwen Ruby from her bag.

Larpraz took hold of the Ruby and raised it high above his head. He began to chant.

"Oh, Coridwen Ruby

Gem so bright

You bless us again.

With your presence this night.

Give power to Ninor.

For a year and a day

When again, we'll go hunting

On an elven bloomday."

When he had finished the Ruby rose into the air and exploded in a burst of light.

Dana watched in awe as it spread through the homes and businesses of the village.

"Come!" Said her father, "We must go see the council."

"Wow! What a day it's been, such an adventure." She thought.

She told her father excitedly about the Craven Marsh Dragons, the tricky Sprites of the Emerald Lake, and the mighty Idris Fomor.

She had completely forgotten about her bloomday.

That is, until…

"SURPRISE, HAPPY BLOOMDAY."

All the villagers jumped up and shouted…

Aoife rushed up to hug her, Princess Lucy was next.

"Sorry for knocking you over before," she chirruped.

Bran came forward grinning widely.

"Hey great job today," he said. "I hope the fire helped you dry off, oh, and sorry about the rock-slide."

Dana stared at him, her eyes wide.

Bran smiled and winked. "You didn't think you'd be sent out alone did you. Shh, it's a secret." He said raising a finger to his lips.

"Every elf gets a shadow; we always look out for each other."

Dana's mother and father come over and hugged her.

Elder zPret stood in front of the crowd and clapped his hands for quiet.

"Young elf Dana Idesan, today you faced a great challenge, and you succeeded in bringing back the Coridwen Ruby.

For this Ninor thanks you."

A cheer rose from the crowd!

"It is with great pleasure that we, accept you as our newest council member."

Another loud cheer erupted from the room.

"There remains only one last thing to say," he shouted above the noise.

"LET'S PARTY!"

With that the music began and everyone started to dance.

Dana sat down and smiled. Everyone remembered she thought as she drifted off to sleep.

THE
END

About The Author

Gary O'Brien is a dad of 3 children and works as a Sales Executive for a software company in Ireland. Growing up in Dublin Ireland, Gary used to spend days reading and dreaming of being a writer.

In 2020 that dream became a reality with the publication of his first book in the Elves of Allaria series, Danger in the Lightning Sands - A Test of Friendship.

This is book 2 in that series. If you enjoyed reading The Coridwen Ruby - A Coming of Age, please leave a review on Amazon.

To sign up to our mailing list to get notified of new upcoming books in this series, send an email to:

DrAki.Writing@gmail.com

Or Follow us on facebook @Gary.OBrienAuthor · Author

Printed in Great Britain
by Amazon

57157634R00050

The Coridwen Ruby by Gary O'Brien.

Published by Gary O'Brien

© 2021

For permissions contact:DrAki.Writing@gmail.com

Illustrated by Caitriona Dalton

ISBN: 9798592209550

Imprint: Independently published